Lulu Frost is the pen name of Angela McAllister, who has written over sixty books for children of all ages, including several award winners. She lives with her family in an old cottage in Hampshire, England, and loves to spend time in her garden, where she grows flowers of every color of the rainbow.

Lorna Brown studied fine art painting in college and works as an artist and illustrator from her cottage in Somerset, England. Lorna also works as an animal therapist, so she has the perfect balance between art and her love of animals and the outdoors!

Fran Brylewska studied animation at art college, where she met her husband David. After illustrating children's pre-school magazines, Fran formed her own illustration company with David in 1997. They now work and live in Dorset, England, with their children Zac and Anya.

Sandy Creek
NEW YORK

An Imprint of Sterling Publishing
387 Park Avenue South
New York, NY 10016

Text © 2012 by Parragon Books Ltd
Illustrations © 2012 by Parragon Books Ltd

This 2013 edition published by Sandy Creek.

ISBN 978-1-4351-4916-8

Manufactured in Shenzhen, China
Lot #: 2 4 6 8 10 9 7 5 3 1

06/13

The Pink Princess

Princess Sophia
loved pink.

She had a bright
pink room ...

with a plump pink bed.

She had a huge pink closet full of frilly pink dresses.

She had rosebud pink shoes ...

and a pink tiara.

One day, Princess Chloe came to play at the palace for the very first time. She brought Pink Princess Sophia a lovely new necklace! But there was only one problem ...

"It's not pink!"
cried Princess Sophia.

"This is a very kind gift," said the King.

"Look how it sparkles in the sun," said the Queen.

Princess Sophia peered at the necklace.
It really was beautiful. But it wouldn't go with
her pink dress, pink shoes, or pink tiara!

"Come on, Princess Sophia," said Princess Chloe.
"Let's go play!"

Princess Sophia put the necklace in her pocket, and, with a nod from the King and Queen, she followed Princess Chloe into the palace gardens.

Princess Chloe picked a beautiful
red flower.

Princess Sophia looked at her
in surprise. "Are you sure we're
allowed to pick flowers?" she said.

And she skipped away, through the garden, picking differently colored flowers for her hair as she went.

Princess Sophia looked at the pink flower, but then she noticed some bright purple blossoms.

She picked some of the blossoms and put them in her hair, just like Princess Chloe.

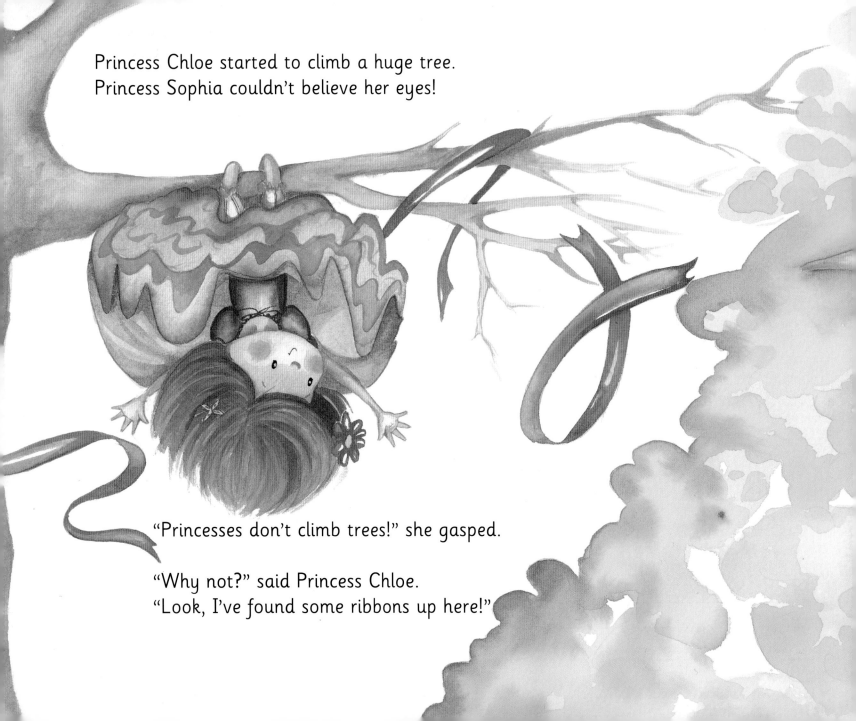

Princess Chloe started to climb a huge tree.
Princess Sophia couldn't believe her eyes!

"Princesses don't climb trees!" she gasped.

"Why not?" said Princess Chloe.
"Look, I've found some ribbons up here!"

Princess Sophia recognized the ribbons of a kite she had lost, streaming like a rainbow in the breeze. She climbed up into the tree and felt like a bird among the bright green leaves.

Princess Chloe untangled the ribbons
and tied one around her waist.
She tied one for Princess Sophia, too.

"Now catch me if you can!" said Princess Chloe.
She scrambled down the tree, and
Princess Sophia followed closely behind.
Princess Sophia giggled as leaves caught
in her hair.

Princess Chloe ran to the meadow. "Look, ladybugs!" she said, kneeling down to see them.

"Princesses shouldn't crawl about getting dirty!" said Princess Sophia.

"How else can you see all these amazing creatures?" asked Princess Chloe.

Princess Sophia knelt down beside her.

"Look," she said. "There
goes a grasshopper, too!"

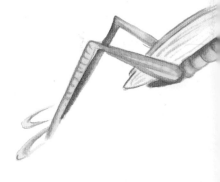

Something pink glinted between the trees.
"Let's explore over there!" said Princess Chloe.

They ran to fallen petals floating on a lily pond.
Princess Chloe dabbled her fingers in the water.

"I suppose princesses can get wet, too?" laughed Princess Sophia.

"I'm making friends with the fishes," said Princess Chloe.

A dragonfly fluttered over the pond,
its colorful wings catching the sun.

It landed on Princess Chloe's
outstretched hand. Princess
Sophia jumped back nervously.

Princess Chloe
whispered to the
dragonfly, "She
doesn't like anything
that isn't pink."

The dragonfly's
wings drooped.

"Yes, I do!" shouted Princess Sophia. "I like the bright flowers and the green leaves, and the blue pond and this shimmering dragonfly with the most gorgeous, most colorful wings I have ever seen!"

The dragonfly stretched out
its wings proudly.

"Why don't you try on your new necklace now?" asked Princess Chloe. She helped Princess Sophia fasten the delicate clasp.

Princess Sophia admired her colorful reflection in the pond. Then she smiled.

"I don't mind that it's not a pink necklace ..." she said.

"Because I'm not just a pink princess any more!"